MAC
and the
MAGIC

drawings by Will Sheldon
story by Marriott Sheldon
color by Karen Urgelles

For -
Court and Lindsay
Will and Taylor
and James

Mac and the Magic
Copyright ©2020 Marriott Little Sheldon

drawings by Will Sheldon

www.marriottartist.com

ISBN-13: 978-1-79475-299-3

Published in the United States

Mac and his friends live on planet Mico.

Life on Mico is magical!

EVERYTHING they
dream happens!

Mac dreams of being a magician.

Ike invents fantastic things!

Jaina and Juno go on safari.

Sal explores space.

Pete performs.

Everyday Mac and his friends
dream BIG adventures!

They are pirates on ships

and knights in armor.

They play games like hockey

and hide-and-seek.

And they all dream of ice cream!

One day Mac and his friends see two strange creatures.

The creatures say a weird word,

"Kuno!"

Then they disappear!

Mac asks the king but
he doesn't know.

The king loads the cannon,
just in case.

Mac and his friends are afraid and THINGS GO WRONG!

Mac forgets his magic tricks.

Ike's inventions explode, **kaBoom!**

Jaina and Juno get lost in the jungle.

Sal's spaceship crashes. (but he's ok)

Pete panics!

The king hides in the castle.

Even their pets act odd and
no one feels like playing.

"Oh Noooooooo!"

they yell.

"The strange creatures stole the magic!"

They all run around doing different things.

Mac makes voodoo dolls.

Ike invents an alien trap.

Jaina and Juno stampede!

Sal installs force fields.

Pete faints.

The king fires the cannon,

BOOOOOOOM!!!

Huge rocks crash down causing chaos!

"INVASION!!!" they all scream.

It's only a meteor shower.

A meteor hits Mac's head and he remembers

EVERYTHING they dream happens!

Mac starts dreaming.

He dreams and

dreams and...

Poof! There's a huge mirror.

Mac invites his friends and the strange creatures to see his new magic trick.

They all arrive and look in the mirror...

"Ike, Jaina, Juno, Sal and Pete," says Mac,
"meet Kuno and Cal!"

"HA!" They all laugh and make funny faces.

Life on Mico is magical again!

There's a party at the castle and Pete performs perfectly.

The king gives Mac a medal for his magic trick.

They play games and eat ice cream in all different flavors.

Now everyday Mac and his friends dream AMAZING adventures!

They skateboard up waterfalls

with crowns on their heads.

They are pirates and knights on oceans of ice cream!

And when strange
creatures appear

nobody screams.

They just dream

more flavors of ice cream!!!

Mac and all the strange creatures were drawn by **Will Sheldon** when he was 4 years old while living in Michigan and Hong Kong. He drew from his imagination and would often draw his dreams before breakfast. Will received a BFA in Illustration from School of Visual Arts in New York City and is now an artist living in Manhattan.

Marriott Sheldon, Will's mom, was inspired to write Mac and the Magic based on Will's drawings. She is an artist and creative coach. Marriott received a BA in English from UNC-CH and a MFA in Painting from William Paterson University. She sees creativity and dreams as powerful ways to create our reality and change the world.